T0132301

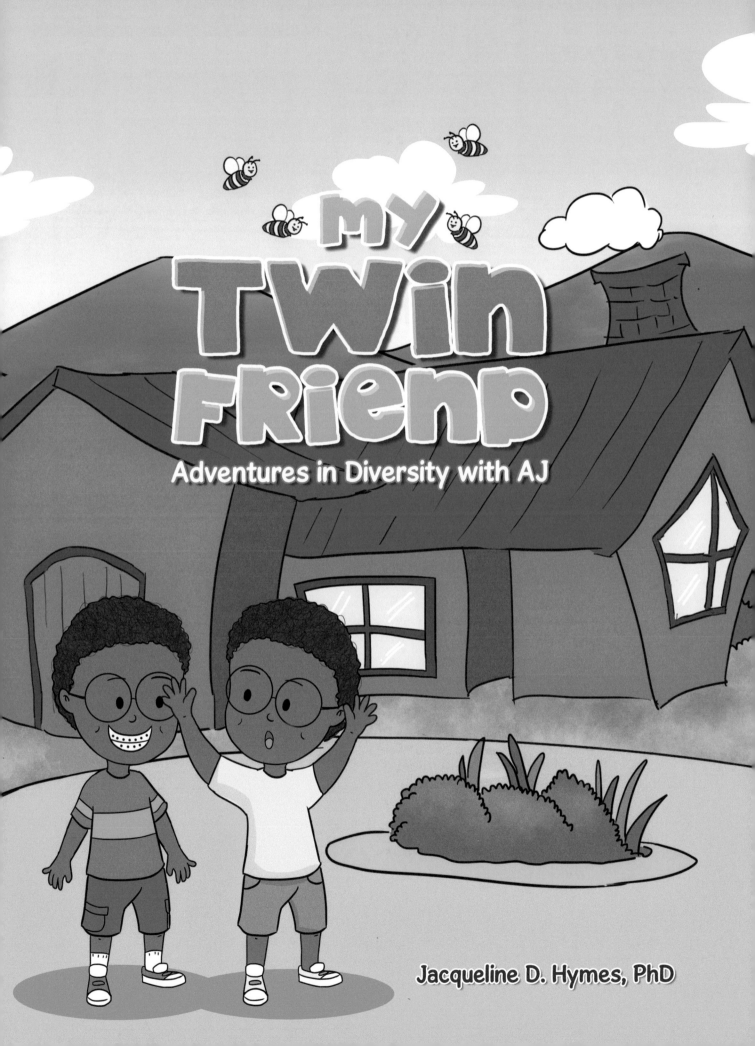

My Twin Friend

Adventures in Diversity with AJ

Jacqueline D. Hymes, PhD

Order this book online at www.trafford.com
or email orders@trafford.com

Most Trafford titles are also available at major online book retailers.

 www.trafford.com

North America & international
toll-free: 844 688 6899 (USA & Canada)
fax: 812 355 4082

Our mission is to efficiently provide the world's finest, most comprehensive book publishing
service, enabling every author to experience success. To find out how to publish your
book, your way, and have it available worldwide, visit us online at www.trafford.com

Because of the dynamic nature of the Internet, any web addresses or links contained
in this book may have changed since publication and may no longer be valid. The views
expressed in this work are solely those of the author and do not necessarily reflect the
views of the publisher, and the publisher hereby disclaims any responsibility for them.

Any people depicted in stock imagery provided by Getty Images are models,
and such images are being used for illustrative purposes only.
Certain stock imagery © Getty Images.

ISBN: 978-1-6987-0281-0 (sc)
ISBN: 978-1-6987-0280-3 (e)

Library of Congress Control Number: 2021920120

Print information available on the last page.

Trafford rev. 12/09/2021

My TWiN FRienD

Adventures in Diversity with AJ

Hi, my name is AJ, and I want to be your friend. We can go on a lot of fun adventures and learn new things along the way. Sound okay to you? Great!

Before we go on our adventure, I want to tell you about my favorite subject. It's called DIVERSITY. Do you know what that means? Di-ver-si-ty.

Well, diversity is this big word adults use to describe how different we are from one another. The main thing to remember is that diversity covers everything that you may find different from you—from where you go to school to where you practice religion, from the color of your skin to the color of your eyes, from the number of brothers and sisters to the number of pets. It covers everything. That's important—knowing that other people are different from you and that it is okay. Remember that you are different from them, too.

Now take a moment and think about this. What if everyone in the world was the same—looked the same, acted the same, talked the same? How much fun would that be, and how could we tell who was who?

Want to have fun learning about diversity with me? Let's go!

FRIDAY

It was officially Spring break. AJ and his best friend Blake will spend time together at AJ's house during Spring break. "See you tomorrow," says Blake. AJ smiles.

Saturday

Mom goes to wake AJ. To her surprise, he is putting on his shoes. "I will brush my teeth after I eat. I don't want my food to taste like toothpaste," he said. Mom smiles. "I made your favorite today— French toast then, we will pick up Blake," said Mom.

Mom and AJ arrive at Blake's house. The kids play while the parents talk. Mom says, "The boys will be fine. They are best friends and always get along."

Once home, Blake and AJ run inside to play a new game. The first few hours are fun. They each pick different games to play. They played games until the wee hours of the morning.

Sunday

The boys eat breakfast then race to see who picks the first game. AJ wins, but Blake decides he rather ride the bikes. AJ is disappointed, but he lets Blake have his way.

Later, they disagree over what movie to watch. AJ let Blake pick. Although AJ was not happy, he enjoyed the movie and then fell asleep. AJ dreams about having a friend who is exactly like himself, a twin friend who loves to do everything he wants to do. They never disagree. AJ dreams about how much fun that would be.

Monday

AJ wakes up and sees Blake under the blanket. "Blake," he shouts. "Get up. Let's go eat." AJ wants French toast but knows Blake wants pancakes. Blake had not budged. It was as if he had not heard his name. AJ shouts, "WAKE UP BLAKE!"

Blake pops his head out. AJ looks surprised. He thought he was looking in a mirror. AJ sees AJ instead of Blake. They are now twins! AJ whispers to himself, "I have my twin friend!"

What do you want for breakfast?" AJ asks. "I want French toast because that's my favorite," Twin Friend replies. AJ smiles.

AJ asks Twin Friend what he wants to do after breakfast. Twin Friend says, "I want to do whatever you want to do, AJ. "Video games," yells AJ. Wow, thought AJ, this is going to be fun! Twin Friend picks AJ's favorite games; the boys play video games late into the night. AJ was very, very happy!

Tuesday

AJ asks Twin Friend what he wants for breakfast. "French toast," he responds. We had that yesterday, but French Toast is good on any day, thought AJ.

AJ wants to get on the trampoline but asks Twin Friend what he wants to do. "Let's do whatever you want to do," he replied. "Okay, let's go," says AJ.

At first, it was fun. AJ soon got bored. Twin Friend did the same tricks as AJ and never anything different.

"What do you want to do next?" asks AJ. He was dreading Twin Friend's answer. "Whatever you want," says Twin Friend. AJ rolls his eyes and says, "Come on."

They ride bikes. It was fun at first, but Twin Friend only did the tricks AJ did.

Mom asks the boys where they want to go for dinner. Twin Friend says, "I want to go anywhere AJ wants to go." AJ rolls his eyes. "Why, Blake, that's so sweet of you," Mom says. AJ wonders why Mom called Twin Friend Blake.

That evening, AJ plays on his phone. Twin Friend stands next to AJ to watch him. AJ gets annoyed with Twin Friend and goes to bed early that night.

The Next Day

"Why did I want a twin friend," AJ says out loud. "Being different is more fun," he continues. AJ shakes Twin Friend awake. "Leave me alone silly," says the voice under the blanket. Did he just call me silly?" AJ thought. Twin Friend was showing his personality. "You do know how to have fun, Twin Friend," said AJ through his laughter.

The voice asks, "Who is Twin Friend?" AJ looks confused. Twin Friend's voice was different. He made it sound like Blake. He'll still be boring, and I miss Blake, AJ thought.

"TWIN FRIEND, TWIN FRIEND, AJ wants his TWIN FRIEND," sings the voice.

AJ looks up with amazement. "BLAKE," yells AJ. "BLAKE, BLAKE, BLAKE," he screams.

"Why did you call me Twin Friend," laughs Blake? "I don't know," said AJ. "I think I was still dreaming. What day is it?" AJ asks. "Come on, AJ, let's eat. You are light-headed and acting very weird. You need food," says Blake. "We can have French toast for breakfast," he adds. AJ screams, "NOOOOOOOOOO! Let's have pancakes." AJ is very, very happy.

Now let's talk about what we learned about diversity by answering a few questions.

1. What does diversity mean to you?

2. How are you different from your best friend?

3. Why did AJ want a friend just like himself?

4. Why did AJ get bored with his Twin Friend?

6. Why was AJ so happy that Twin Friend was a dream?

7. Would you like your own Twin Friend? Why?

8. What did you learn about diversity today?

Printed in the United States
by Baker & Taylor Publisher Services